For Mom, Dad, Todd, and Traci. Thank you for
still putting money in my birthday cards.

Sheep Dog and Sheep Sheep
Copyright © 2019 by Eric Barclay
All rights reserved. Manufactured in China.
No part of this book may be used or reproduced in any manner whatsoever
without written permission except in the case of brief quotations
embodied in critical articles and reviews. For information address HarperCollins Children's Books,
a division of HarperCollins Publishers, 195 Broadway, New York, NY 10007.
www.harpercollinschildrens.com

Library of Congress Cataloging-in-Publication Data

Names: Barclay, Eric, author, illustrator.
Title: Sheep Dog and Sheep Sheep / Eric Barclay.
Description: First edition. | New York, NY : Harper, An Imprint of
HarperCollinsPublishers, [2019] | Summary: An oblivious sheep wants to be
the best sheep protector around, but unbeknownst to her, Sheep is being
steadfastly guarded by a patient sheep dog.
Identifiers: LCCN 2017057326 | ISBN 9780062677389 (hardcover)
Subjects: | CYAC: Sheep—Fiction. | Sheep dogs—Fiction. | Dogs—Fiction. |
Farm life—Fiction.
Classification: LCC PZ7.B2357 Sh 2019 | DDC [E]—dc23 LC record available at
https://lccn.loc.gov/2017057326

The artist used pencil and Adobe Photoshop to create the illustrations for this book.
Typography by Jeanne Hogle
18 19 20 21 22 SCP 10 9 8 7 6 5 4 3 2 1
❖
First Edition

ERIC BARCLAY

SHEEP DOG AND SHEEP SHEEP

HARPER
An Imprint of HarperCollinsPublishers

This is Sheep. She loves to dance.

She knows all kinds of fancy dances.
Like the Wildflower Dance . . .

the Mud Puddle Dance . . .

the Get This Spider Off of Me Dance . . .

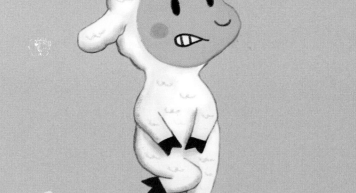

and, of course, the Pee-Pee Dance.

Dancing makes her very happy.
And when she's happy, she closes
her eyes.

And when she closes her eyes, she
bumps into things. Usually trees.

But one day she bumped into something that wasn't a tree. It was a someone. A very hairy someone.

"Holy begonia!" she said. "Who are you?"

"I'm the sheep dog," the someone replied. "I watch the sheep."

"Well, I'm a SHEEP sheep. I watch sheep, too. Everyone knows I'm an expert at watching sheep.

"I don't see how you can be much of a sheep watcher with all that hair in your eyes.

"But I can fix that for you. Be right back!"

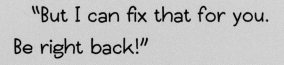

She skipped off toward
the farmhouse.

Just then, Sheep Dog spotted an eagle overhead. It was looking at Sheep like a mouse looks at cheese.

The eagle dived . . .

. . . but Sheep Dog told him to vamoose.

Sheep found Sheep Dog waiting for her outside the
farmhouse, and she tied his hair into a pretty bow.

"Now you'll be able to see the sheep," she said.
"Except you're still missing something VERY important.
Be right back!"

Sheep Dog looked around. It was true he could see a little better with his hair pulled up. There was the shed . . .

and the apple tree . . .

and the coyote . . .

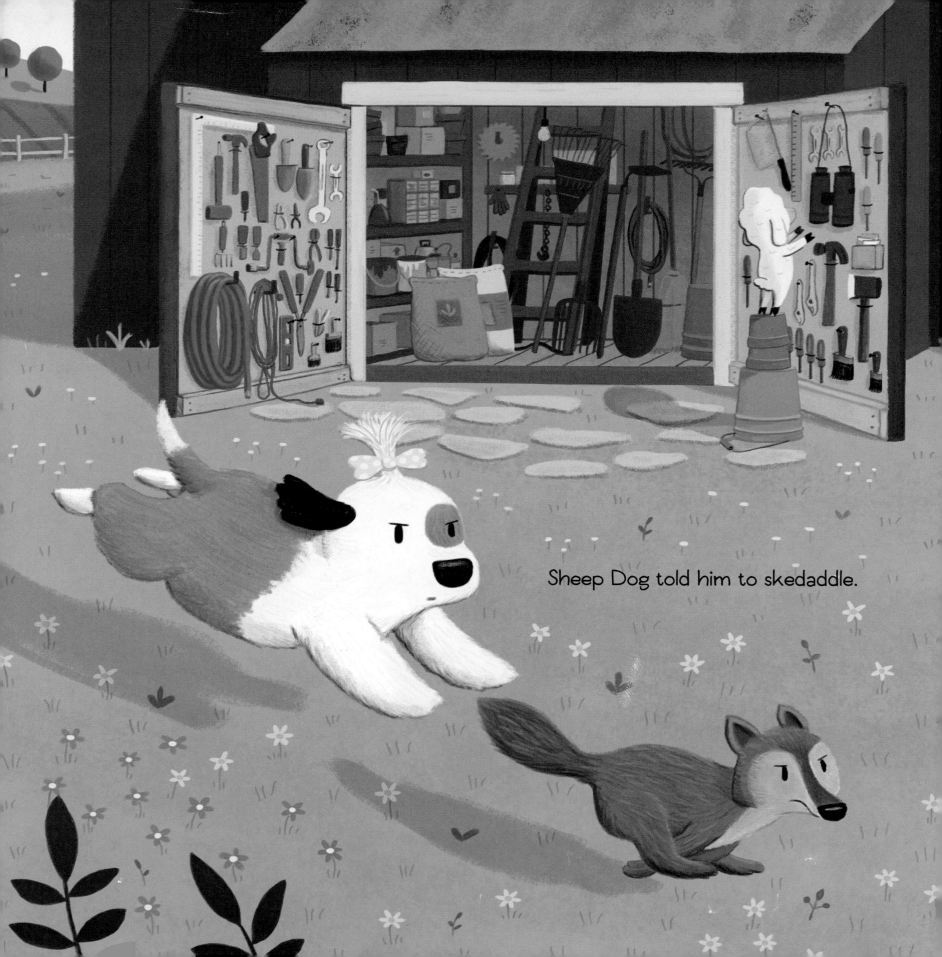

Sheep Dog told him to skedaddle.

Sheep returned with some binoculars. "Here you go!" she said. "Now you'll be able to keep a sharp eye out for eagles and coyotes.

"Now, I don't suppose you have a map under all this hair, do you?"
Sheep Dog shook his head no.
"Well, you're going to need a map so you won't get lost. Be right back!"

She danced her way toward the old truck to retrieve a map.

The dance made her very happy. She closed her eyes.
And because her eyes were closed, she couldn't see that . . .

But Sheep Dog did.

Sheep kept on dancing.

She had some extra-fancy moves.

Like most of Sheep's dances, this one ended with a bump on the head. But she had meant to do that.

Really.

Sheep fished the map out of the glove box and handed it to Sheep Dog.

"You're all set! You've got a hair bow so you can see, binoculars to keep an eye out for danger, and a map so you won't get lost."

Sheep thought for a moment.
"Now all we need are the sheep."

She looked around.
Not a sheep in sight.

She borrowed Sheep Dog's
binoculars. Still no sheep.

She unfolded the map.
Yep, they were definitely in
sheep country.

"Where are all the sheep?"
she asked.

"You're the only sheep,"
Sheep Dog said.

Oh.

Sheep sat down and thought about being only a sheep and
not a sheep sheep. And when she thought, she got very still.
And when she got still, she got very quiet. Thinking could do that.

Finally, Sheep Dog spoke. "Maybe you're not a sheep sheep. Maybe you're a DOG sheep, and your job is to watch the dog."

After a moment, Sheep replied, "Well, OF COURSE I'm a DOG sheep!

"Everyone knows I'm an expert at watching dogs."